DOCTOR GENIUS
AND
THE MAD SCIENTISTS

THE TIME WARP VIRUS

Clive Gifford

Designed by Russell Punter

Illustrated by Geo Parkin

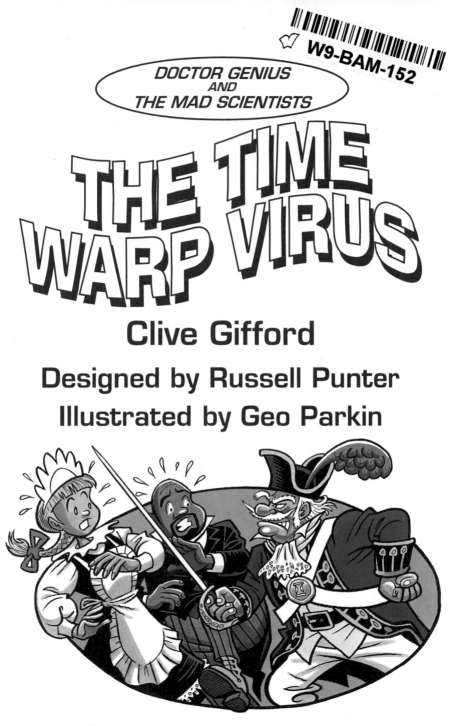

Series Editor: Jane Chisholm

CONTENTS

2 Meet the Mad Scientists

4 The Virus Starts...

6 Breakfast is Served

8 False Icons

10 Following Leads

12 A Clinical Decision

14 Feat of Clay

16 The Servant Problem

18 A Warped Idea

20 Orchard of Intrigue

22 Rogue's Gallery

24 Plane Sailing

26 Welcome to Castle Warp

28 Apple Pi(e) Puzzle

30 The Hidden Message

32 Mirror Maze

34 Sweet Solution

36 Vault of the Virus

38 Hardware Hassle

40 Optical Illusion

42 Just Desserts

44 Dr. Genius Explains...

MEET THE MAD SCIENTISTS

The Mad Scientists are a team of great brains and little common sense. They are dedicated to using science for good to make the world a better, safer place. The intrepid leader of this amazing gang is Dr. Genius.

In their rambling collection of laboratories and workshops, the Mad Scientists are constantly tinkering away with new ideas and inventions. But they rarely finish them off. Why? For three important reasons.

One: they're not interested in becoming rich. Provided they have enough money to buy the occasional piece of new equipment, then they're happy.

Two: they're too scatterbrained to follow a project through.

Three: the most important reason of all, they're far too busy solving mysteries, uncovering dastardly plots and overcoming evil superbrains, to finish their own scientific work.

To the Mad Scientists, the most important task is to stop criminal masterminds from using science for their own evil ends.

Each member of the team is particularly clever in one area of science and fairly stupid in others. For example, brilliant biologist, Rosie Bloom, probably wouldn't know one end of a car from the other. The selection of computer disks below will give you an idea of their different interests.

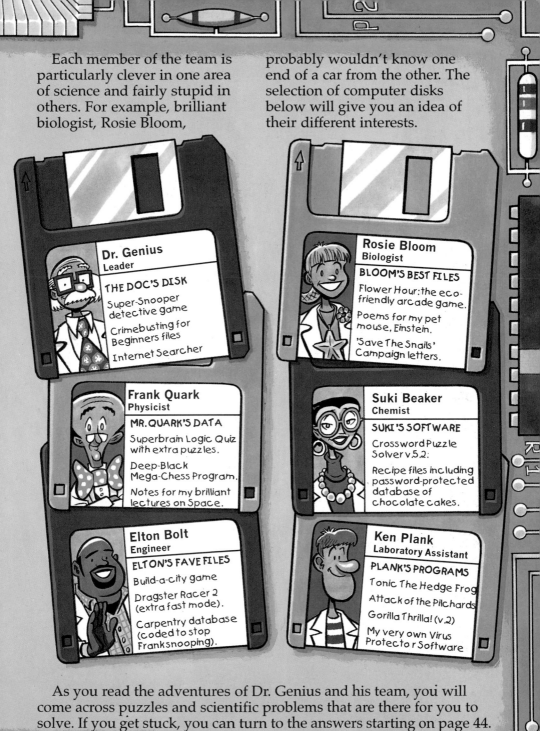

Dr. Genius
Leader

THE DOC'S DISK

Super-Snooper detective game

Crimebusting for Beginners files

Internet Searcher

Rosie Bloom
Biologist

BLOOM'S BEST FILES

Flower Hour: the eco-friendly arcade game.

Poems for my pet mouse, Einstein.

'Save The Snails' Campaign letters.

Frank Quark
Physicist

MR. QUARK'S DATA

Superbrain Logic Quiz with extra puzzles.

Deep-Black Mega-Chess Program.

Notes for my brilliant lectures on Space.

Suki Beaker
Chemist

SUKI'S SOFTWARE

Crossword Puzzle Solver v.5.2:

Recipe files including password-protected database of chocolate cakes.

Elton Bolt
Engineer

ELTON'S FAVE FILES

Build-a-city game

Dragster Racer 2 (extra fast mode).

Carpentry database (coded to stop Franksnooping).

Ken Plank
Laboratory Assistant

PLANK'S PROGRAMS

Tonic The Hedge Frog

Attack of the Pilchards

Gorilla Thrilla! (v.2)

My very own Virus Protector Software

As you read the adventures of Dr. Genius and his team, you will come across puzzles and scientific problems that are there for you to solve. If you get stuck, you can turn to the answers starting on page 44.

THE VIRUS STARTS...

One Sunday afternoon, things went very wrong in the Mad Scientists' labs. A computer virus had infected their main computer, resulting in mayhem.

"I never knew the computer ran the fire sprinklers," shouted Suki, trying to switch the water off.
"And I didn't realize some buffoon had computerized our windows and doors," cried Elton.
"Sorry. My fault," muttered Frank, struggling with the unruly front door. "I was trying out a security system for when we go away."
"Look, even our computer-linked clock is racing back in time," scowled Suki.

"What exactly is a computer virus?" asked Rosie desperately trying to catch flying test tubes with her fishing net.
"It's a computer program deliberately written to damage the data and programs inside a computer," Ken replied. "And, what's more, I think this one might be the work of Silica Stevens."
"Who's she?" asked Elton.
"Only the biggest troublemaker the computing world has ever known," explained Ken.

"Oh, I wish Dr. Genius was here!"

"The odd thing is that Silica Stevens reformed over a year ago. She's even written a book on disabling her viruses. I have a copy somewhere," added Ken, searching feverishly.

"Oh, I was just using your book for an experiment," piped up Frank. "I was testing different items to see if they could build up a charge of static electricity to attract strips of paper."

"I was using three items in my experiment," Frank droned on. "A balloon, a piece of amber and a machine called a van de Graaff generator. The book was underneath the one item that I hadn't yet charged with static." After pausing for breath, Frank was about to continue, when the front door suddenly knocked him to the floor.

WHAP!

Stifling a smirk, Suki helped a dazed Frank to his feet.
"So, where's my book, then?" Ken cried.
"After that thump, I can't remember," groaned Frank.

Can you spot the missing book?

BREAKFAST IS SERVED

Alittle later, Frank came to his senses, grabbing a book from under a block of amber.

"Here it is!" he cried, waving Ken's book. "You see, I'd rubbed the pink balloon on my coat and, as our cat found out, I'd already switched on the van de Graaff generator. Did you know that this machine uses a rubber belt moving against two rollers to create lots of static electricity..."
"Shut up Frank!" the others chorused.

Flicking through his book, Ken discovered the virus was Silica's most powerful program, and that she called it the Time Warp Virus. "Please disable the virus before the computer's clock travels back to 7am," begged Suki.
"Why?" asked Frank.
"Elton's breakfast-maker is joined to the computer," Suki replied.
"So what?" snapped Ken.
"Too late. It's seven already!"

Yeeeeooooowww!

Elton reached out for the plug to his breakfast maker just as scalding hot coffee from the machine poured itself all over his outstretched hand.

"Run your hand under cold water," frowned Suki, swerving to avoid two boiled eggs which hit the wall behind her.

"Doesn't Silica Stevens work at the Computer Addicts' Clinic?" Rosie wondered out loud. No one answered. The others were too busy dodging pieces of breakfast to reply.

Ken continued to search for clues. "I've got it! 67 is the code," he cried, typing the number in.

Decimal	Binary						
	64	32	16	8	4	2	1
10 =	0	0	0	1	0	1	0
20 =	0	0	1	0	1	0	0
40 =	0	1	0	1	0	0	0
80 =	1	0	1	0	0	0	0

"Oh, no, the number doesn't work!" moaned Ken desperately. "Computers sometimes use the binary number system. Perhaps the number should be entered in binary," suggested Suki. "You can convert the decimal number into binary, if you use this chart," she continued, digging out a table of binary numbers from beneath a pile of toast.

Can you work out the binary number equivalent of 67?

7

FALSE ICONS

K en looked in despair at the screen which showed a large plant beginning to wilt. 100011 was the right number, but the virus still hadn't stopped. In fact, it looked like they'd hit another level of security.

"What are those?" asked Rosie, pointing at the little boxes arranged around the plant.

"They're called icons. You can click on them to perform different tasks," replied Ken.

Suddenly, Dr. Genius rushed in carrying a surfboard. "I've just been surfing the Internet on the spare computer," he guffawed. "Really, Dr. Genius. Now's not the time for jokes," scowled Rosie.

"I'm not joking," replied Dr. Genius, pulling the plug on Elton's breakfast machine and wedging the surfboard against the door to keep it from opening and slamming shut. "I'd just heard about this Time Warp Virus and so I decided to search for more information. Before I lost the link, I learned that the virus has been made harder to disable. Did you know that the dying plant is a countdown timer?" The others stared at the screen in horror.

"You mean we've got until the plant dies to find the right code?" asked Ken. "Yes, and the icons you need to click on are all to do with photosynthesis," Dr. Genius added. "What on earth's that?" asked Frank.

"It's how a plant makes food, silly." replied Rosie. "Plants need carbon dioxide which they get from the air, so click on the air icon in the top corner, Ken."
"Okay, Rosie."

"And plants need water, so click on the bucket of water icon," insisted Suki. "Plants also need a substance called chlorophyll to turn carbon dioxide and water into food," instructed Rosie.

"There's no chlorophyll symbol," muttered Ken. "No, but the leaves contain chlorophyll," said Suki.

"Good, that worked. Now, what else?" asked Ken.

CRASH! The surfboard hit the floor, the door flew open and there stood a delivery boy with a large basket of apples.
"Are you the Mad Scientists?" he gasped. They nodded.
"These are for you, then," the boy added, dropping the basket and fleeing before the Scientists could ask him any questions.
"Apples? What do we want with apples now?" exclaimed Frank.

"Strange apples as well. Look, parts of them aren't ripe."
"I guess they were kept in the dark," mumbled Suki.
"That's it. That's the last thing a plant needs to make food," Rosie squealed, hopping up and down.
"Just one more icon to click on Ken," she cried with excitement.

Can you guess which icon Ken must select?

9

FOLLOWING LEADS

Ken selected the sunlight icon and the screen cleared. "Plants need light," said Rosie. "The computer's showing the right time," declared Dr. Genius with satisfaction. "The virus has been stopped." The scientists punched the air in excitement. Unfortunately, Ken jumped so high he thumped the sprinklers back on. It took hours to mop up all the mess.

The next morning, the Scientists found a sleepy Ken printing out a long list of all the computers affected by the Time Warp Virus. Ken explained that the reason viruses were so dangerous was because they could spread so easily from one computer to another. "This is the floppy disk that carried the virus onto our machine. Whose is it?" he asked. "Er, um. Mine I'm afraid," blushed Elton. "I got it free with *Nostalgia Yesterday* magazine." The scientists read the disk's label. "Well, if the virus had won, we'd have been without a computer, that's for sure," said Frank. "Why don't you and Rosie contact the magazine, Elton," suggested Dr. Genius. "We'll go and visit Silica Stevens at the Computer Addicts' Clinic."

A little later, Elton rang off looking very disappointed. "Any luck?" Rosie asked. "No, I just left a message."

On the other end of the line, a large, blustery figure listened to Elton's message and cursed through tightly-gritted teeth.

"Not only have my insolent servants deserted me, but those Mad Scientists know about the Time Warp Virus already, and I've only just finished my trial run. Who'd have thought they'd read *Nostalgia Yesterday* ?"

The large figure took a gulp from his pewter flagon of mead and started to calm down. "At least some new servants will be here soon. I must get my virus-infecting machine ready fast. I just need to untangle these leads so I can connect the keyboard... Now which one of these plugs is joined to the blue one?"

Can you help the Baron decide?

A CLINICAL DECISION

The Scientists were shown into the clinic by a polite robot. "Take us to your leader," joked Dr. Genius. The others all groaned. "Ahhh, poor joke from sci-fi films. Tell me when did you start watching too much TV?" asked the robot in a soothing voice. Dr. Genius's cheeks turned red.

The robot stopped asking embarrassing questions and introduced itself. "I am Sigmund Droid. Dr. Rom who runs the clinic is busy trying to find us a new home. Apart from me, Silica Stevens is his only helper. She was his first successful case, you know."

Sigmund Droid lead the scientists around the clinic. "Dr. Rom uses different techniques to cure each patient."

"This one here is called regression therapy. The patient starts with the latest computer, then is given an older one."

"Gradually the patient receives older and older machines until, like Eric here, he is almost cured."

And in this room is Dr. Rom's latest method. He's very excited about this. He calls it actual reality.

You mean letting patients out into the real world?

Er, yes.

"Instead of using computer databases, we encourage visits to libraries," said Sigmund Droid. "What about video games?" asked Suki.

"Easy. We replace computer sports with real sports. It's much healthier than sitting in front of a computer all day," said the robot.

"But what about games like Tiger Wars and Gorilla Thrilla?" quizzed Ken. "Oh, we just take the patients to the zoo, instead."

The robot lead them over to the Craft Corner and introduced them to Silica Stevens. They explained that they wanted to discuss the Time Warp Virus. "Little scruffy for such famous scientists, aren't you?" said Silica, unimpressed. "Haven't you ever seen Einstein's hair?" protested Dr. Genius. "And isn't he a little young...and handsome," Silica cooed at Ken. "I'm not a real scientist. I'm a lab assistant," Ken stammered. "I've been learning a lot about science myself," said Silica.

"So, if you really are who you say, then you can solve a scientific problem, can't you?" Silica grabbed some clay and walked over to a bowl of water. "The density of clay is greater than water, so an ordinary lump will sink if l drop it in. So how do I make it float?" she asked.

"Easy," said Frank in a bored voice, wandering off before the others could ask him to explain. "I think I can do it," smiled Ken slightly nervously.

What does Ken do?

13

FEAT OF CLAY

Ken had the clay afloat in no time. Dr. Genius started to explain. "When an object is in water, it displaces water, or pushes it out of the way. If the weight of water the object pushes is greater than the weight of the object, then the object will float."

Suki scratched her head. "But clay is heavier than water."
"Ah, but by stretching it into a bowl shape, Ken made the clay take up a much larger space. Now, it pushes away a lot more water, more than it weighs," Dr. Genius replied.
"Very good," mumbled Silica.

Displacement is what makes big ships float.

What's this line?

That's the plimsoll line. It shows how low a ship can safely float in the water without sinking.

Okay, okay. You're definitely scientists, so I'll tell you what I know. When I was still a troublemaker, I sold a copy of the Time Warp Virus to a man who called himself the Baron. The codeword we used was Revenge. I try not to use computers now but, when I heard about my old virus being used, I did some investigating.

"Would you mind helping to disable the virus on all the infected computers?" asked Dr. Genius. "No, not at all, especially if this hunk can stay and help too," gushed Silica, smiling at Ken. "Must I?" pleaded Ken desperately. "Yes, Ken. You must. *Don't think of yourself, think of the planet*," chanted Dr. Genius.

"The Mad Scientists' motto," added Suki. Ken's shoulders drooped as Silica led him away. "Ken, eh? Now, that's a nice name..."

Frank appeared holding up a basketball vest. Suki sniggered. "Very funny. All I did was hand over a memory chip and the kid insisted I take the cap and vest." "But, Frank, you're not supposed to encourage them. They're already computer addicts,"

frowned Suki. "It was only a chip!" cried Frank. "As a punishment, wear them for the rest of the day," snapped Dr. Genius. "Now let's get home."

Can you unscramble the message on the Internet?

THE SERVANT PROBLEM

Meanwhile, Rosie and Elton were alone at the labs, looking through a CD ROM all about failed crimes.

The forger who couldn't spell was funny.

Hey, look at this!

Failed criminals file 72%

Behind The Times Baron
Baron Timothy Gribbledyke Warp, a would-be super criminal who's so old-fashioned that he's always refused to learn anything about computers. Every time he almost succeeded in committing a crime, a computer in some way or other thwarted him. In his last term he confided to another prisoner his ambition to rid the world of all computers.

T.G. Warp

more

While they were reading Baron Warp's file, Rosie and Elton were disturbed by a polite cough.

Who are you?

Sorry to startle you. I'm Roland Butter. Until yesterday, I was Baron Warp's head waiter.

My name's Andy Withnails, the Baron's ex-handyman.

And I was Baron Warp's cook, Mrs. Beecham.

The servants calmed down and began to go through their story again, but this time more slowly. They explained that when they discovered the Baron's dreadful plans, they decided to leave and go to the police.

"You've seen the police?" "Yes, about an hour ago. We even spoke to the Police Chief, who said the station was in turmoil because their computers had been infected with the Time Warp Virus. She recommended that we visit you."

"We know the Chief very well," said Rosie, her eyes narrowing in suspicion. "If she really sent you, she would have given you the answer to this puzzle..."

IF $\triangle = 180°$ AND $\square = 360°$ $\pentagon = ?$

Can you guess the coded answer?

A WARPED IDEA

The servants handed over a note from the Police Chief containing the answer to Rosie's puzzle. Then they told Rosie and Elton all they knew about Baron Warp's plans.

"The Baron loathes science and technology so much that I had to cut out any news about them from his newspaper before giving it to him," sighed Roland Butter. "And when I asked if I could have a vacuum cleaner instead of a broom, he fined me a week's wages," exclaimed the handyman. "So why's he had a computer built for him?" asked Elton.

The servants explained that it was the Baron's ambition to get rid of the world's computers by infecting them with the Time Warp Virus, and that he needed a computer to carry this out...

"But what's the point of it all?" asked Elton.
"We don't exactly know. He did say something about revenge."
"Remember the CD ROM Elton? Every time Warp tried to commit a crime and become a famous supercriminal, he was stopped by a computer," said Rosie.

"You Scientists should hurry, before it's too late," urged Mrs. Beecham. "All we know is that those computer disks he sent out were what he called 'his trial run'."

"We've drawn you a couple of maps showing you where the castle is," said Andy Withnails. "Once you get to the orchard near the castle, Baron Warp's gardener, Old Growbag will be waiting for you. He's a little ancient, but he's on our side and he'll tell you how to get into the castle."

"Aren't you coming with us?" asked Rosie.
"Oh no. We must go back to the police station and fill in reports," insisted Roland Butter firmly.

I wish we'd used my dragster.

But think of the exercise you're getting...

After the servants left, Rosie hid one of the maps and scribbled out a coded note for the other Scientists. Then they leapt on their bicycles and the two of them set off for Castle Warp.
"Which way should we be going?" asked Rosie.

"According to the map, we should be heading on a compass bearing of 315°."
"But what direction is that, Elton?"

What compass direction do you think is at 315°?

Rosie and Elton quickly reached the orchard near Baron Warp's castle. "I wonder where that old gardener is?" said Rosie, scratching her head.

"Right here, Madam," rasped an unfamiliar voice. Rosie and Elton jumped. "Sorry to startle you. I'm George, but the other servants call me Old Growbag."

"Hope you didn't eat the special clues I sent you," said Old Growbag mysteriously. Rosie and Elton shook their heads, trying to figure out what he meant. "I don't think they know what I'm talking about," muttered the gardener. "Lucky I sent that extra note to explain..."

Then the gardener handed Rosie and Elton some old servants' clothes to disguise themselves and led them to a secret passageway into Baron Warp's castle.

These clothes are so uncool.

And a little tight. The previous butler must have been tiny.

Back at the Mad Scientists' labs, Suki, Frank and Dr. Genius were puzzling over Rosie's message.

"Oh, I wish she'd just leave a simple, uncoded note for once," moaned Frank. "Be quiet, Frank. Rosie pinned it on your solar system chart, so it's probably a clue," frowned Suki. "It must be about the planets," declared Dr. Genius.

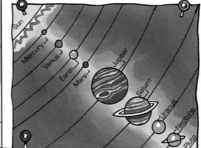

But if you want to get into the castle, you need to look like servants.

Now I'd better be off to join the others at the police station. Good luck!

ARBNO	EGNO	RNEUD	OT	LSCTAE
Earth	Mercury	Uranus	Venus	Jupiter

SMEOU	'SAWPR	APM	GCEA
Neptune	Mars	Saturn	Pluto

Can you decipher the message from the clues Rosie has left?

ROGUE'S GALLERY

Meanwhile, Rosie and Elton crept into the castle and were amazed at what they saw.

What an incredible place. It's like a museum. I'll make a plan of our route.

Do you want to borrow my pen?

No thanks. I've got something of my own to write with.

As Rosie explained what she was doing, Baron Warp was elsewhere in the castle, struggling with an enormous silicon chip. "If only I'd got the measurements right in the first place. This would never have happened if I hadn't had to use metric measures."

The Baron dragged the memory chip down some stone stairs. With this chip in place, his Revenge Machine would be complete. He noted some muddy footprints at the entrance to the secret passageway and thought he'd better investigate.

Avoiding a number of traps and pitfalls, Rosie and Elton advanced deep into the heart of the castle. They entered a room lined with paintings, all of Baron Warp, but couldn't get the door ahead to budge, even after Elton had thrown his considerable weight onto it.

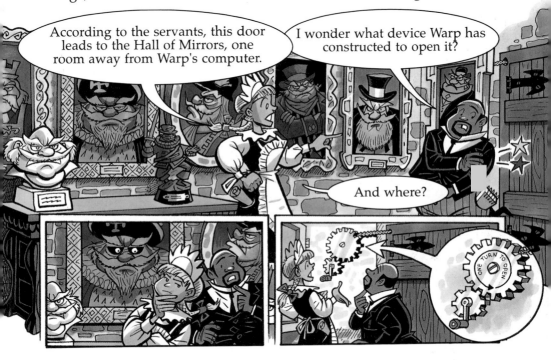

According to the servants, this door leads to the Hall of Mirrors, one room away from Warp's computer.

I wonder what device Warp has constructed to open it?

And where?

ONE TURN TO OPEN

Behind a painting, the Baron was spying on the two Scientists. "Intruders, eh? This is war!" he hissed, rushing off.

A few minutes later, Rosie found what looked like the solution behind another of the paintings of Baron Warp.

"The two gears are linked, but the smaller one has half as many teeth. It looks as if the bigger gear needs a whole turn to open the door. So how far should we turn the smaller one?" asked Elton.

How far do you think Elton should turn the smaller gear?

23

PLANE SAILING

Elton moved the first gear half a turn and moaned in dismay, "The door hasn't moved." "That's because you have to turn the smaller gear two whole turns to make the bigger one move one turn," a huge booming voice echoed around the castle.

The two Scientists turned and leapt back in horror as Baron Warp suddenly appeared. He pushed past them and turned the handle around twice. Slowly, the door cranked open. Then the Baron confronted them with a look like thunder.

Waving his cutlass, the Baron demanded that Elton and Rosie turn out their pockets. Eyeing the contents suspiciously, he seized Elton's notebook, but allowed Rosie to reclaim her piece of paper.
"What are you doing trespassing on my property?" thundered the Baron.
"We're the new servants you requested, er, Sir," explained Elton none too convincingly.

"I think not," roared the Baron. "A map of my castle, eh? If you think you can stop me from getting revenge and being taken seriously as a top criminal, you are much mistaken."

Warp chased them high up into the East Tower of the castle and into a small room at the top. Terrified, Rosie and Elton slammed the door behind them. But they heard the sound of a key in the lock and footsteps retreating back down the stairs. They were trapped.

The pair scoured the room for a way out, but without success. Suddenly, from a tiny window, they spotted Dr. Genius and the others approaching the castle. "Maybe we can get a message to them," suggested Rosie. "How are we going to throw a piece of paper all that way, and so far left of the window?" sighed Elton.

"Paper engineering can help us," shouted Rosie in triumph, launching a paper plane made from her notepaper. Elton grinned, unfolded the plane, carefully wrote a message and then remade it. "Now all we need to do is fold this rudder to make the plane turn," said Rosie.

Do you know the correct way to bend the rudder to make the plane turn to the left?

WELCOME TO CASTLE WARP

The paper plane turned gracefully to the left and glided down to Dr. Genius, Suki and Frank. The three Scientists carefully studied Elton's message.

"We must get to the computer quickly to disable it in time," said Frank. "But don't you think we should rescue Elton and Rosie first, Dr. Genius...Dr. Genius?" But Dr. Genius wasn't listening. He had turned over the piece of paper and was sniffing the other side.

"Dr. Genius, are you mad?" asked Frank. "No, but you're a lemon," snapped Dr. Genius, tired of Frank's pompous ways. "Phone Ken and Silica and get them to head over here too. We're going to need all the help we can get to foil Baron Warp and his plans," continued the Mad Scientists' leader.

The Mad Scientists stared at the amazing contraption in front of the castle door.

"Typical of Baron Warp to have an old-fashioned lock," said Suki. "Still, it's all about gears, so Frank should know what to do."

"Oh, it's too practical for me," said Frank. "I hate to say it, but I wish Elton were here."

"Well, I know that turning one gear will turn another the opposite way," said Suki proudly.

"We can turn this bottom one to move the others," added Frank.

"But we must be careful," said Dr. Genius. "Turning the top cog clockwise will cut the rope and we'll become food for crocodiles."

"True. But if we turn the top cog the other way, we can get the door open," pointed out Suki.

Which way should they turn the first cog?

APPLE PI(E) PUZZLE

Frank turned the first gear clockwise and watched as the other gears clanked, whirred and slowly moved. The last gear turned the other way and, with an almighty groan, the bolt slid back and they were able to heave the door open.

"We've done it!" cried Suki in excitement.

"Quick. Let's get inside before Baron Warp spots us," urged Frank.

Back at the Computer Addicts' Clinic, Ken and Silica had just finished sorting out all the virus queries when they received the urgent phone call from the others. Silica hurried Ken onto her motorcycle and sped off through the town.

Racing at incredible speed, taking short cuts down narrow alleyways and across ditches, they soon reached the Mad Scientists' labs.

Quivering and shaking from the hair-raising journey, Ken opened the lab door and spotted a note on the floor. Silica rushed to open it.

Dear Sirs and Madams,

A couple of months ago, I began to suspect Baron Warp was up to something. Just in case it turned out to be useful, I found out the phone number of his new computer, and stored it in a place where the suspicious Baron would never look - on apples growing in the orchard. These were the same apples I sent you a couple of days ago. I left paper numbers on my apples so, when the rest of the apple ripened, the unripe part under the paper would show the number. I left a coded note on the basket as an extra clue. The first five numbers go in descending order and the second four numbers equal pi. Hope this helps.

George 'Old Growbag' The Gardener.

Deep in his castle, Baron Warp was preparing himself for his greatest hour. "Soon, the virus will gain me my revenge. Then, I'll wager, no one will doubt my claim to be a supercriminal, ha, ha, ha!"

Back at the labs, Silica feverishly delved through the basket and collected all the apples she could see with numbers on them. "Where's the ninth one, Ken?" she asked. Ken's mouth was too full to speak, so he just handed back what was left of the apple.

Staring at the apples, Ken and Silica tried to puzzle out the meaning of George's note.

What is the correct order for the apples?

THE HIDDEN MESSAGE

Silica solved the puzzle and whooped with delight.

"Pi equals 3.142! So, the phone number to contact Baron Warp's computer must be 98765 3142."

Jumping back on the motorbike, Silica and Ken raced over to Warp's castle. As they got near, they took a wrong turn and reached an old jetty by the river.

S.S. WARP

Hey! That must be the Baron's boat.

Look at all the things he plans to load into it.

Well, we'd better do something about it, just in case the Baron is planning to escape.

WARP JETTY
TRESPASSERS WILL BE
KEEL HAULED!

Ken levered open a can of paint, the same shade of yellow as the boat. He quickly slapped the paint over the black line on the side of the boat.

"What are you up to?" asked Silica. "Nearly finished," said Ken, opening a second can of paint and brushing a black line higher up on the side of the boat.

"Is it really the time for graffiti, Ken?" scowled Silica. "Oh, this isn't graffiti, this is genius!" declared Ken with the widest of grins.

Back in the castle, Frank, Suki and Dr. Genius were scratching their heads over which way to go next.

Which way to the computer room?

What are you doing Dr. Genius?

Just trying to get Rosie's message, you lemons.

Why is Dr. Genius heating the paper?

You see, Rosie drew her map with lemon juice. When it dries, it's invisible, but heat it gently and the writing can be seen. It's all to do with chemical reactions, but we don't have time for that now.

Using Rosie's map, Frank, Suki and Dr. Genius soon reached the gallery and then entered the Hall of Mirrors.

Look at this!

How do they do that?

"It's all about curved mirrors you see," Frank started to lecture. "A curved mirror bends light, which..." But Dr. Genius interrupted sternly.

Just then the Scientists spotted two blue things. "Those are light sensors. They're sensitive to bright light," explained Dr. Genius. "According to Elton's note, they both need to be hit at once to open the door into Warp's computer room."

"But we only have one light, and these flat mirrors are in the way," sighed Suki. "Ah, yes, but light can bounce at an angle off a mirror. That's how a periscope works," explained Dr. Genius. "My calculations indicate that the current arrangement of mirrors isn't satisfactory," said Frank pompously. "But we can turn these mirrors 45° at a time," replied Dr. Genius.

Suki sketched a quick map of the mirrors. "Good work," congratulated Dr. Genius. "Now, I think we only need to move two mirrors 45° each to get our light to hit both sensors at the same time."

Can you see which mirrors should be moved, and in which directions?

SWEET SOLUTION

Deep in the castle, Baron Warp was setting in motion the final stage of his fiendish plan. He started the Time Warp Virus using a laptop computer joined to his giant machine.

masterplan programs

ENTER CODEWORD

R E V E N G E|

Soon, all computers all over the world will be disabled. No need for me to be here any longer. It's off to my lovely seaside retreat, ha, ha.

Meanwhile, the Scientists had managed to open the door, but they'd found another obstacle. "How could we tell there'd be another door behind it?" wailed Frank, picking up an old lantern. "Look, here's another light." "And here's another light sensor," declared Dr. Genius.

The Mad Scientists tried to shine both their lights on the sensor, but this time without success.

"Hang on, didn't Elton's note say something about needing light like amber to trigger one of the sensors?" gasped Suki. "Yes, of course," remembered Frank. "Amber is yellow!"

"But how do we make lights yellow?" pondered Dr. Genius. "l know. Chocolate wrappers!" hollered Suki.

She emptied a bag of chocolates onto the floor. "Yes, you can shine a light through these cellophane wrappers and they will act like a filter. They're translucent, you see, which means that some light will pass through them," lectured Frank smugly.

"Hang on, I'm afraid there's no yellow wrapper," Suki sighed. "No, but when I paint I use blue and green to make yellow," said Dr. Genius, greedily grabbing two chocolates and popping them into his mouth.
"No, you mix blue with yellow to make green," insisted Suki.
"Oh, that's it," said Dr. Genius, as if he had known all along.

"But light works in a different way from paint," explained Suki triumphantly. "With the right wrappers, we can make yellow light by putting a different wrapper over each of the two lights. And we have the right wrappers here."

Which two wrappers will turn the light yellow?

The sensor flashed. "Red and green light mixed together make yellow," explained Suki. The door slid open and the Scientists stared in horror at Warp's fiendish machine. "That's what happens when you mix up your measures," said Dr. Genius.

Frank explained how the optical character reader scanned numbers off the paper roll and fed them into the computer. The computer then phoned each number and, once linked to a computer on the other end of the line, downloaded the destructive virus.

"We need to act fast to stop Warp's machine." "But it's protected by a row of laser beams." "How strange. The off switch seems to be broken. It's powered by a battery, but part of the circuit has been removed. Turn out your pockets onto the floor everyone. We need something that will conduct electricity to bridge the gap," said Frank.

LASER CUT-OUT SWITCH

GAP IN CIRCUIT

"Any ideas Dr. Genius?" But Dr. Genius was still struggling with the chewy chocolates in his mouth.

MMMmmmurrghh!

Unnnggg!

Phhhhhoooooolllpp!

Dr. Genius spat out a gold filling and sat down dazed. Suki checked to see if he was okay, but Frank was busy staring at the objects on the floor. Suddenly he realized he'd found something...

CHALK-O Chalks

Can you guess which object will conduct electricity?

TIME WARP VIRUS ON

HARDWARE HASSLE

Frank placed Dr. Genius's gold filling into the circuit. It worked perfectly and in no time the laser beams had disappeared. "It was lucky that Dr. Genius's filling was a really old one, made mainly of gold. Gold is one of a number of metals that conduct electricity," said Frank. "Good job you can't resist chocolates, eh?" remarked Suki.

"Ugarr, ngguunngg" replied Dr. Genius. "Now, how do we stop this machine?" asked Frank.

Meanwhile, the Baron had made it as far as the jetty and was loading his boat with supplies. He was amazed at just how much he could squeeze into the tiny vessel. When the level of water in the river almost reached the black line on the side, Warp jumped into his boat. Adjusting the rigging, he set sail for his secret seaside retreat.

Back in the computer room, the Mad Scientists had tried everything they could think of.

It's impossible to stop this optical character reader.

I can't push this mouse.

I'm not heavy enough to press a key.

We've failed. We can't stop the program.

"We may not be able to stop the program, but we might be able to feed it a very interesting phone number," interrupted Dr. Genius, switching off the phone. "That was Ken and Silica. They're outside the castle. That basket of apples contained the number of Baron Warp's computer: 98765 3142."

"So, if we could get that number scanned and inputted...the computer would contact itself...and infect itself with the virus!" declared Frank.

Frank and Dr. Genius tried to write on the roll of paper being scanned. But the optical character reader was too fast and their pens weren't thick enough to make big enough numbers. Then Suki noticed that one of the numbers was the same as the number of Warp's computer, except for two digits...

Meanwhile, from the orchard on the hill, Silica had spotted the boat sailing along the river. "Warp's getting away," she moaned. "Oh, I wouldn't count on it," sniggered Ken.

What do you think will happen to the boat?

OPTICAL ILLUSION

From his tiny boat, Baron Warp spotted Ken and Silica running up to the river bank. He waved sarcastically and shouted, "Goodbye landlubbers." By the time Baron Warp noticed that the boat was sinking, it was too late...

"You see, I repainted the plimsoll line higher up the boat, so that the Baron would think he could load it with even more equipment and it would still float," explained Ken smugly. "Very clever, but he's still getting away," scowled Silica.

Baron Warp had managed to leap off the sinking ship and swim to the other side of the river bank.
"My wealth gone and my plans in ruins," he cursed. "I had better use Escape Plan B."

Back in the castle, Dr. Genius had a brainwave. "*Eureka!* Your new number 14 shirt is just what we need," he said, pushing Frank onto the roll of paper. "Keep still!"
Before he could struggle to get off the paper roll, Frank was plunged head first under the optical character reader.

Heeellllp!

Frank limped back to the others. "I hope that was worth it," he muttered breathlessly. "Oh, I think it was," replied Dr. Genius with a smile, as he watched the on-screen clock racing back to zero. "Look, Warp's computer has infected itself with the virus." Suki and Frank looked on in amazement as Warp's machine started to break down. In no time at all, it had ground to a halt. "Great! Now, let's go and rescue Elton and Rosie," said Suki.

Sopping wet, the Baron headed away from the river and reached the edge of some woods. "Good thing l hid an alternative means of transportion," he muttered to himself.

Baron Warp moved aside some branches to reveal a carriage, and a horse grazing peacefully. "Right, Bess, off to my hideout to plot the downfall of cars and televisions next," he urged the horse.

As the Baron climbed into the carriage, twitched the reins and roared "Giddy-Up!", Old Growbag, hiding behind a tree, stifled a chuckle. "Whhoooaaarrhhhh!" screamed Baron Warp as the horse and cart raced around in tight circles. By the time it eventually stopped, both the evil Baron and poor Bess felt faint with dizziness.

Can you see why the cart went round in circles?

JUST DESSERTS

Ken and Silica reached the clearing and laughed when they saw what was happening.

"I thought you'd left, Old Growbag?"

"I almost had. But then I spotted the Baron's carriage hidden in this field. Apart from his boat, it's the only vehicle the Baron owns. So I thought it just as well to sabotage it."

"Well done!"

"It certainly looks as if the Baron's going around in circles!"

Some time later, after the Baron had been taken to the police and all the infected computers had been fixed, there was a great reunion back at Castle Warp. The castle, which had been confiscated in compensation for the Baron's crimes, was now in the hands of the servants. They'd been put in charge of modernizing it and running it as a tourist attraction.

You've certainly done a great job in such a short time.

Well, Silica, Sigmund Droid and their computer clinic patients did most of the work.

Oh, it was the least we could do, after we were allowed part of the castle to rehouse our clinic.

"And without you, Mad Scientists, we'd never have been able to put a stop to the Baron's plans," announced Roland. "Ah, but let's not forget the real hero," piped up Dr. Genius. "If George here hadn't discovered the number for Warp's computer and, later, stopped Warp from escaping..."

"I'll ring for some cakes," Old Growbag mumbled, shaking a small silver bell.

"By the way, I've been meaning to ask you all... Whatever happened to Baron Warp?" inquired Suki.
"Oh, you'll see," smiled Andy Withnails mysteriously.

Baron Warp!

He's just called Tim now.

Thank you Tim, that will be all. Now, scram!

He got 20 years community service for his crimes. He's helping to keep the castle in order.

Foiled by blasted computers and scientists again!

Ha! Ha! Ha!

DR · GENIUS EXPLAINS · · ·

Pages 4/5

Ken's book was under the block of amber. Amber is the fossilized remains of resin from certain trees which has hardened over millions of years. The amber was the one item that Frank had not yet charged with static electricity. So, unlike the van de Graaff generator and the balloon, it had not attracted the pieces of paper.

Some objects, such as balloons and amber, can get charged with electricity simply by being rubbed with wool or fur. This action transfers electrons to the object which becomes charged with static electricity. This static attracts objects, but only the lightest, such as feathers and small pieces of paper, actually move.

van de Graaff generator

Pages 6/7

The binary equivalent to the number 67 is 100011. Binary is a number system which uses only ones and zeros, unlike the decimal system we use every day which uses the numbers zero to nine.

We know that in the decimal system the units column goes from zero to nine. When one is added to nine, the units column is full and one is put in the tens column. Binary works in exactly the same way, except that a column becomes full when it has more than one in it. The chart on page 7 helps convert the decimal number 67 into a binary figure.

64	32	16	8	4	2	1
1	0	0	0	0	1	1

$64 + 2 + 1 = 67$ $67 = 1000011$

Computers use binary because they can convert ones and zeros into electrical signals, which they can send around the computer quickly and easily.

Pages 8/9

Ken should click on the sunlight icon. Sunlight energy, carbon dioxide and water are what plants need to make sugar as food. They do this in parts of their leaves called chloroplasts, which contain a substance called chlorophyll. The whole process is called photosynthesis. Water, containing dissolved minerals and nutrients, is drawn up from the ground through the roots of a plant. Carbon dioxide gas is taken in from the air through a plant's leaves. The water and carbon dioxide are combined to form sugar and oxygen. The plant doesn't need oxygen and so it lets it go back into the air.

Pages 10/11

The yellow connector is joined to the blue plug, as the picture shows.

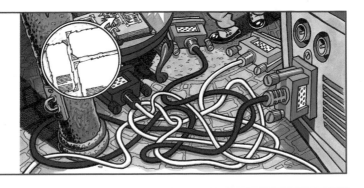

Pages 12/13

Ken makes the clay float by shaping it into a bowl.

When an object is placed in water, it pushes aside, or displaces water, to make room for itself. The water which the object displaces pushes back up against the object.

The size of the upward force on the object depends on the amount of water displaced. The more water displaced, the bigger the force. If the upward force is as big as the object's weight, the object will float in the water. If the force is smaller, the object will sink.

As a lump, the ball of clay only displaces a small amount of water and so sinks. But, made into a bowl shape, the clay displaces much more water. The upward force of the displaced water is equal to the weight of the clay, so it floats.

Pages 14/15

The Internet message reads:

SOMEONE CODENAMED REVENGE BROKE INTO MY DATABASE AND STOLE ALL THE TELEPHONE NUMBERS TO CONTACT THE TWO MILLION MOST IMPORTANT COMPUTERS IN THE WORLD. CAN ANYONE HELP ME GET THIS INFORMATION BACK OR I'LL LOSE MY JOB.
SECURESYS1 @ TOP GOVTCOMP

The message was written as a mirror image, with all the Es and As switched around. (To decode a mirror message, place a mirror next to it.)

Pages 16/17

The answer to Rosie's code question is 540° - the number of degrees in the angles of a pentagon (any five-sided shape).

You can see this more easily if you divide the pentagon into three triangles. The angles in any triangle add up to 180°, so
$3 \times 180° = 540°$.

Did you see the clue on page 12, where the boy with the abacus left his working out?

Pages 18/19

Elton and Rosie are heading Northwest. A compass face is divided into 360°, just like a circle. North is at 0° or 360°, South is at 180°, East 90°, and West 270°. 315° is halfway between West and North, hence Northwest.

Did you spot the compass sign being carried on page 14?

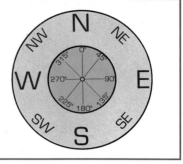

Pages 20/21

The message that Rosie left says:

GONE TO BARON WARP'S CASTLE MAP UNDER MOUSE CAGE.

Each of the words is jumbled up but Rosie also jumbled up the order of the words. She did, however, link each word to the name of a planet in the solar system. The words in Rosie's message are in the same order as the planets are from the Sun. The Mercury word EGNO, or GONE, is first as Mercury is nearest the Sun. The Pluto word, GCEA, or CAGE, comes last as Pluto is farthest away from the Sun.

Pages 22/23

The smaller gear, with half the teeth, has to make two complete turns to turn the larger gear one full turn.

Gear's teeth engage

Pages 24/25

The tail rudder should be bent to the left. This will make the paper plane veer to the left.

As you will know from walking into a wind, air can put strong forces on objects in its way. A plane is designed for the air to flow smoothly over it without it putting much force on the plane. But if the tail rudder is bent outward, the air pushes against it with a bigger force. Because the force is only on one side of the plane, it causes the tail of the plane to turn.

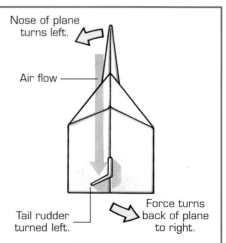

Nose of plane turns left.

Air flow

Tail rudder turned left.

Force turns back of plane to right.

Pages 26/27

The first gear must be turned clockwise to make the fourth and last gear turn the other way. When gears are connected, turning one will turn the next one in the opposite direction.

Pages 28/29

The correct number is 98765 3142. The first five numbers are in descending order, which means from the largest down to the smallest. The last four numbers equal the mathematical symbol Pi (shown as π) which equals 3.142 when rounded up.

Pages 30/31

Dr. Genius is heating the piece of paper to see Rosie's map drawn in lemon juice.

The piece of paper Rosie made into a plane was the same piece on which she drew her map of the castle. Dr. Genius could smell the lemon on the paper and suspected that Rosie had used lemon juice as an invisible ink. When gently heated, lemon juice reacts chemically. It turns brown and becomes visible.

Pages 32/33

Moving mirrors E and G, as shown in the diagram, would mean that the light hits both sensors. Light bounces off angled mirrors and can be directed in the same way as it is in a periscope.

Did you spot the periscope blueprint on page 15?

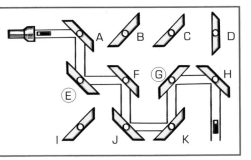

Pages 34/35

The red and green wrappers will together make yellow light when each is placed over a light source. Red, green and blue are the primary light shades. They can be mixed together to form other, secondary, light shades.

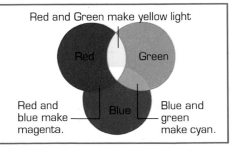

Red and Green make yellow light

Red and blue make magenta.

Blue and green make cyan.

Pages 36/37

Dr. Genius's very old filling, which is mainly made of gold, will conduct electricity.

Most substances that conduct electricity are metals. Copper, for example, is a very good conductor and, because it is commonly available, it is used for most electrical wiring.

Substances that don't conduct electricity, like wood or plastic, are called insulators.

Pages 38/39

Baron Warp's boat will sink. Ken repainted the plimsoll line (which shows the lowest the boat can safely sit in the water) much higher up the boat's hull. This means that the boat is sitting much lower in the water than is safe. As soon as the boat starts moving through the choppy waters, the tops of the waves start to fill the boat with water, which makes it sink.

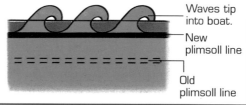

Waves tip into boat.

New plimsoll line

Old plimsoll line

Pages 40/41

The cart races around in circles because Old Growbag replaced one of the cart's wheels with a much smaller one.

Both wheels are fixed to the same axle and so both must turn around the same number of times. The circumferences of the wheels are different. This means that, as the horse pulls the cart forward and the axle turns, the side of the cart with the larger wheel will move a greater distance than the side with the smaller wheel. This has the effect of making the cart go around in a circle.

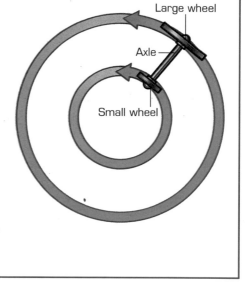

Large wheel

Axle

Small wheel

First published in 1996 by Usborne Publishing Ltd, Usborne House, 83-85 Saffron Hill, London EC1N 8RT, England.
Copyright © 1996 Usborne Publishing Ltd.

The name Usborne and the device 🏆 are Trade Marks of Usborne Publishing Ltd. All rights reserved.

Printed in Great Britain   UE
First published in America, March 1997.